TALES FROM THE
SILVER STATE V

Compiled by Steven Fey, these stories are presented unedited, as fresh and original as when they were first written down.

These stories are works of fiction. Names, places, characters, and incidents are the products of the respective author's imagination, or are used fictionally. Any resemblance to actual places, events, or persons living or dead, is purely coincidental.

ISBN-13: 9780998972022***

ISBN-10: 0998972029***

E-book ISBN: 978-0-9989720-3-9***

Printed in the United States of America

TheFeyCow, Las Vegas, Nevada

Tales from the Silver State IV is set in Palatino Linotype, an oldstyle font noted for being easy to read, and used in many books.

DEDICATION

This anthology is dedicated to the memory of John Hill, friend and mentor to many Las Vegas writers, who passed away suddenly before he could see his story here published. You are missed, John.

TALES FROM THE SILVER STATE V

The Authors:

- John Hill
- Wayne Baker
- Edward Riepe
- Jay Hill

TABLE OF CONTENTS

PLEASANT DREAMS
A Short Story

By John Hill

Joseph Gibson, 38, a successful advertising executive, arrived at his beautiful home in L.A.'s Laurel Canyon, afraid he'd be late for dinner since he just come from his first therapy session. I just hope I don't have the same dream again, he thought, but at least this time, I'll have someone to talk to about them, maybe even make them stop. His son, Billy, 7, and daughter, Emily, 4, ran to him, all hugs and excited talk about their day. His beautiful blonde wife, Abby, met him with a smile and kiss, negotiating her way around the two kids hugging their father. His home was lovely, not big, but nestled perfectly against the canyon wall. Joseph knew he was a lucky man.

"How did the session go?" Abby asked quietly, once kids were out of earshot, as she served lasagna. "Did you like him?"

"Yeah, I like him. He was a little hung up on the fact I've always been a 'Joseph' and not a Joe or Joey, but then when we got into my dream, he was very…understanding. Even had an initial insight…"

Later that night, kids asleep, in their bedroom, Joseph told Abby more. "He kept asking me if somehow down deep I felt I didn't deserve what I have, you, the kids, our nice home, a job I even liked, that it might be the source of the dream." But that night, he dreamed it again.

Joe Gibson, 38, woke up in the alley, cold, aware it had been over two weeks since he'd had a bath, days before he'd even had a 'whore's bath' in the men's room of a nearby stop-and-rob. Shivering, wrapping newspaper around himself, it occurred to him that a part of being homeless was newspapers were blankets. But then, being in the same clothes for days? Alley asphalt for bed linen? Dying for wine, then some food? The full package kit, he knew. He thought about scratching out a cardboard sign and standing on the corner of Hill St. & 7th, hoping to get enough change from traffic for cheap wine, and maybe some food; depressing but probably what he should do.

Joe Gibson had been homeless for the last eight years, ever since his 'fall from Grace,' as he thought of it, when Grace kicked him out of their cheap apartment. She found him drunk again, the want ads for jobs nearby, untouched, when she returned home from work as a waitress. He had his first night being homeless, going to a heated bus station, telling himself that this was temporary. He was sure now every homeless loser started off thinking it was just temporary. Joe made himself get up, tried to remember what time the local soup kitchen opened, where it was, and knew he needed new clothes, or clean ones. He needed everything, actually, then trudged off, into the world, a vague quest for any of the everythings he always needed.

"Hey, Joe, my man," another homeless man said, when he passed him. "You carryin'?" Joe knew the man meant meth, and had to remind him again he was no meth head, but alcohol? Oh, yes…

Joe panhandled on the corner, a cardboard sign, cleaned himself up a little, had wine and food, slept in the alley again that night. Cold.

Joseph Gibson left the agency an hour early two days later, the first time he could get an appointment with Ed Horton, his new therapist, who had said they'd meet once a week unless he had the same dream again, then he'd work him in sooner. And he did.

"So, Joseph," Ed asked, "how long have you had this dream?"

Ed Horton was 58, bald, black, friendly smile, easy attitude. Preferred wearing dark dress slacks, colorful button-down shirts, loafers.

"Seems like…the last few years, at random times," Joseph said.

Joseph at 38 was good-looking with the beginnings of baldness, a hint of gray in his hair, the suggestion of a slight waistline bulge. He knew it would all only get worse, but Abby said he looked very handsome and attractive to her, and that was all he cared about. He always came to therapy from work, so he wore a nice suit and tie. His wife selected them for him. Abby had very good taste.

"The thing about this dream, I've had off and on for years,"

Joseph said, "it's not the same dream. It's me, but I'm always homeless, cold, alone, always. But it changes, a serial dream if you will. And I've had it quite often, lately."

"And you're an otherwise happy man then?" Ed asked.

"Oh, yes. Blessed really. I even like my work and workmates."

"Have you thought about any underlying guilt about your life?"

"Like I unconsciously feel I don't deserve the good life I have? So that's why I dream I have less than nothing, unloved, broke, alone?"

Ed nodded.

"I've thought about it, yeah," Joe said. "But, see, I worked hard, in college, then in advertising. I'm a good man, well, good enough, to get Abby. So I'm not, you know, feeling like I don't deserve my life."

That night, Joseph told Abby about it. Then slept. And dreamed.

Joe woke up in the alley, cold. Los Angeles winters are colder than people realize, but not the homeless who lived there, outdoors. They know. Joe woke up, could smell himself, relieved himself against a wall thirty feet down the alley, made sure he brought his half-full wine bottle with him, taking a long drink from it, started walking. He wasn't sure where he was going, but the hard alley was not letting him sleep, and he was cold. Exercise would help warm him, he hoped.

Joe walked for hours, shuffling along, wine long gone now, until sunrise, which warmed him a little, but he needed coffee, food. He hung around outside a McDonalds, panhandled enough for a coffee, then an Egg McMuffin, sat, watched traffic. Traffic was people who had jobs, places to live, people who loved them, Joe thought.

But not me. Many years ago, so many, he once had those.

Later, he got chased away from a doorway while taking a dump, dodged two guys robbing the homeless, slept in a culvert, shivering.

 Joseph Gibson woke up suddenly in his Laurel Canyon home, seeing his beautiful wife, Abby, beside him, his well-appointed master bedroom, the beautiful view outside his window of canyon greenery.

Abby stirred, then said her sleepy voice, "Again?"

"Yeah," Joseph gasped a little, shaken. "This time I panhandled at a MacDonalds. It was…horrible…I was alone…I had nothing…"

She hugged, then made love to him. He smiled afterwards, and for the rest of that Saturday. Abby once said she loved his smile. He took his daughter to I-Hop for blueberry pancakes, their special time, then as a family, they all went to his son's Little League game. That evening, they had the Rodriguez family over, for a swim in Joseph and Abby's pool. Joseph barbecued hamburgers and hot dogs, afterwards. That night, they were all tired, happy. It had been a great day, until Joseph went to sleep, and had the dream…

Enough of this, Joe Gibson thought, waking up in the culvert, tired of always being so cold. He knew the local places he could be inside and warm up a little, but he knew he now looked "too homeless" so security would ask him to leave. Enough. He'd told himself a thousand times he'd stop drinking but he never did. It was his only escape. Wine blurred, numbed, enabled. But he was tired of it all. Enough, he thought to himself. Was today really the day, he wondered, walking along, going nowhere? Was it really? Joe wondered. Then when he realized that while he needed food, a shower, clean clothes, a job and friends, a life…but what he go after was alcohol; he'd soon make a cardboard sign…again…repeat as needed, he thought to himself.

Then it started raining.

Joe grimaced, getting wet. He'd be soaked. And he'd stay wet. Yeah, enough. Take the risk. And today was the day.

Now.

Just do it.

A second later, without looking, he bolted across the four lane street, full of traffic, into the drivers with lives, hearing horns, knowing he'd never make it to the other side, then felt pain, fear, then nothing.

Joe's body was in a hospital room, and he was an inert mass of wires and tubes. Joe was not conscious. He was in a coma. Joe's brain registered some minor activity, doctors noted, but they also knew he was what the snickering hospital interns secretly called a rutabaga.

"He was apparently homeless," an older doctor said. "All he had was a library card with the name Joe Gibson for an I.D."

"Yeah, that's standard for homeless. You know, with Google and Kindles, who libraries are really for now? The homeless," said a younger doctor. "I always wonder how a guy like this got this way."

"You wonder because you come from a family that loved you, provided support, a home, then college, medical school," said the older doctor. "Other people realize one day they have no family, no friends for sofa-surfing once they lose their jobs, end up on the streets."

"Oh, yeah, you used to volunteer your time at a clinic, didn't you, helping the homeless?"

"Yeah, but it got too depressing," the older doctor said, "or I got too selfish. Roughly one third are homeless because of addiction, another third due to mental illness, the last third are the ones we should help, those who just fell through the cracks and just need a job, a fresh start. But we ignore them all. We'll never knew which one this guy was, but it doesn't matter now. He's in a coma, in a permanent vegetative state, forever, all on the tax-payers. This Joe Gibson will get transferred, some low-rent, permanent care facility, never know the difference. He just sleeps. Come on, we got rounds."

Joe, the dull party at the center of the festival of tubes and wires, heard none of this. He was dreaming, an old, familiar dream he

7

occasionally had.

He dreamed he was called Joseph, not Joe, same age, only he had work. He was even successful. He was an advertising account executive, in a meeting now on a car rental account, and he and the others there were laughing. In Joe's dream, Joseph glanced at his watch. He had to leave early, to go to his session with Ed Horton, his therapist, where he was glad to be able to report his nightmares of being homeless seemed to have stopped. Then he'd hurry home to his Laurel Canyon home, kiss and hug Abby and the kids, read the kids stories at bedtime, then make love to his beautiful wife that night. He didn't much care how much he deserved and how much was luck. All he knew was, unless really bad fortune or terrible judgement happened to him, Joseph Gibson would always have a special, good, happy life.

And Joe dreamed on, not hearing the slow whishes and steady beeps of the medical equipment that would keep him alive for decades, and continue at some level, his ongoing dream, of life, luck, the people he loved who loved him.

"Okay. Well, so long Joe," the younger doctor said to the comatose patient. "Hope you have pleasant dreams, because that's all you'll ever do." And the doctors walked away.

Joe heard none of their talk and he couldn't hear the quiet noise of the equipment that kept him alive and he'd never wake up. He'd just keep dreaming, for the rest of his life.

No one ever could ever medically explain his constant smile.

Abby loved his smile.

THE OLD SHELL GAME

By Wayne Baker

I froze momentarily when I recognized that it was "Lucky Larry" making his entrance and felt hatred for him. Rather than anything he had done, it was the extreme irritation that he evoked in myself and the other patrons. He had even goaded some into making sucker bets with him not for the money wagered but for the possible pure satisfaction of winning a bet from him.

The bar was a warm and friendly place that even evoked memories of a fireplace and large comfortable leather lounge chairs, neither of which inhabited the room. The presence of Larry made it seem like a dark rain cloud had formed.

Larry would proclaim himself to be a winner at either the track or the table or favored by the symbols flying around on the reels of a machine. He would prove his success by waving around a thousand dollar roll of twenty dollar bills. I suspected that fifty ones inhabited the interior. Others scattered around the room would glance up and then ignore him, recognizing that the celebration did not include drinks for the house. It never did.

Larry always claimed that he liked the fast action. What had really surprise me was that I learned he had built his original bankroll operating a shell game in under policed areas along the Atlantic shoreline.

I imagined him standing there at dusk with his small folding table supporting three walnut shells and challenging his victim to pick the one hiding the pea or the marble and win after he had mixed, switched and circled them in a most confusing manner. Somehow the shell picked was always an empty one and Larry had again proved his mastery of sleight of hand.

Upon uncovering this bit of background skullduggery, a sinister plan of revenge began to percolate in my imagination. I was convinced that Larry believed that only one unique method was used by all involved to perform this illusion and he would be completely thrown if any other method was used.

I intended to let the victim, Larry, place a wooden pellet under one of the shells and keep his hand on the shell as he moved it about while following my directions.

To prepare, I picked the walnut shells with the darkest interior that I could find and the interior membrane intact. I glued a tiny but strong magnet inside the shells and prepared a number of wooden balls with the interior scooped out so that the tiniest metal ball bearing would fit snugly inside.

The ball that I intended to use had a golden stripe covering the juncture of the two halves. I made a duplicate that would remain in my pocket until it appeared under a walnut shell that Larry hadn't picked. I prepared other balls with different colors that would exist to help convince that the one placed under the shell to start was the singular one of that design in the game.

And I counted on Larry not looking immediately at the underside of the shell he picked when he was surprised by my revealing another shell as the winner and putting his down or handing it to me when I handed the duplicate ball to him. I would keep reminding him to bear down on the shell he was moving for me so that his hand would become tired and ready to put it aside.

I played the fantasy over and over in my mind of Larry picking up the shell that he was convinced contained the yellow striped wooden ball and handing it to me to take ahold of the duplicate. Needless to say, I had a duplicate shell without a ball to switch as the magnetized shell disappeared.

This plan was so complicated that Larry would never suspect anything other than the old fashioned swindle existed.

Larry, again this afternoon, was being his normal annoying self by waving a bundle of green twenties about as he bragged on his psychic number picking genius at the day's roulette spinning.

"Anybody goat anything interesting to bet on?" he challenged loudly in the quarter filled cocktail lounge. "Something new and exciting to spark the imagination?" He appeared ready to introduce one of his sucker bets.

"Larry," I yelled. "How about a little shell shock?"

"What?" he ask, stopped in his tracks about introducing some new sucker bet, but sincerely filled with curiosity.

"You know intimately about the old shell game, I understand."

"Oh, the old bait and switch. That doesn't interest me.

Your hand could be faster than my eye."

"Thanks for the compliment but I'm willing to let you keep your hand on the shell you pick, hold it down, move it around as directed and pick it up to see if you're focused enough to keep the ball in your court."

"If your magic is as bad as your cliché commentary, I won't have the least bit of a problem. How much do you want to bet? Twenty? Fifty? Maybe a hundred?

"How much money are you holding in your tight little fist?"

"You'll bet me a thousand under those rules?"

"I'll put my money where my mouth is."

"You've got that much on you?"

"I'll have to get it and my equipment out of the car. Can you wait a minute?"

"Oh, for a bet like that I can wait an hour or maybe until next Wednesday."

"I won't keep you that long." I hurried to get my setup out of the car, my shell collection, the small dark brown folding table and the thousand dollars, all in twenties. The money was stuffed under the spare tire. I was back inside in only seconds more than a minute.

Larry was waving his bundle of money, also all twenties that were gripped tightly by a red rubber band. "I thought you might not show up."

"How long would you have waited? No, I'm a serious contender. Call me the shell king, if you like."

"No need for that. You have the money?"

I held up a fistful of my paper money.

Larry looked at the bartender. "Do you have a rubber band that he can put around that?"

"I'll look," the bartender agreed, staring down into whatever assortment of necessities and not were located on a shelf under the bar.

"Never mind. I think I've got one," Larry replied, pulling a rubber band, this one brown, out of a pocket. He took the money from my hand and slid the rubber band over it, sliding it to the center of the bills and tapping the assortment sharply on the bar.

He placed the two packages of money, mine in the brown rubber band on top, on the bar in front of the bartender. "Watch that if you don't mind," he dictated.

I was opening my small table when he told me, "You don't have to do that."

"That's okay. You can see that I have the circles painted on it: one, two and three, so that it will be easier to direct your hand movements."

"We could do that on one of the standard cocktail tables."

This is really kind of my lucky table. With all the advantage I'm giving you in holding onto the shell, I really feel a bit strongly about it."

Lucky Larry didn't object when the table was opened and set up and he had a chance to run his hand over the surface and examine it.

I pulled out two shells from the plastic bag of walnuts, using it for dramatic effect, and placed them on spots one and three marked on the table. Then I pulled out a third shell and held it over spot two. I placed one of the wooden balls under it, the one with a distinctive yellow band, and lowered the shell. "Now if you'll put your finger on it and press down so that there's no way you can see anything under it…"

Larry did as I ask. I had also placed a number of the small wooden balls on the table, each with a colored strip of blue or green. The ball under the shell was the only one on the table with a yellow stripe.

I swept my hand over the assortment of balls, gathering them up and putting them in my left coat pocket. He didn't know that I had a duplicate yellow banded ball in my other pocket.

I gave him the first directions, "Now move the shell with the ball under it to spot one and, using your other hand, the shell from that spot to spot three and the shell from three to two. Keep pressure from your finger on the shell hiding the ball."

I gave him a lengthy tour of moving between spots one, two and three until his patience appeared running low.

"How long are we going to keep this up?"

"You have to give me a chance to move the ball under the shell you are controlling with my mental powers. I have to move it with mind power only from where it is to another shell."

"Yeah, sure," he said with sarcasm and almost a mean-spirited smile.

"If you're tired, you can forfeit the contest and the bet."

"No, I don't think so."

The bartender looked up, breaking his concentration on watching the prize money, "Remember that you declared that if anyone ever won a bet off you that you'd never show your face in this bar again. Just saying. Don't mean to lose your customershsip."

"Is that a word?" Larry glanced distastefully at the barkeep.

"Language evolves and it's evolving right here under our very eyes."

"Okay, Larry," I cut in, "Enough shell sliding. Pick the shell covering the ball."

"This is so easy," Larry chuckled. He raised the shell and was shocked by what he didn't see.

The space under his chosen shell was empty and I quickly raised the adjoining shell, flipping the duplicate yellow banded ball under it with a professional slight-of-hand move. "Here we are," I proclaimed.

I picked up the duplicate ball and handed it to him. This was the critical moment where it would be disastrous if he turned the shell in his hand over and discovered the ball inside.

I counted on his hand being tired from pressing down on the shell while moving it.

So unexpected was this development that he grasped the offered object, allowing me to take the shell that he had been controlling and once in my hand it was replaced by another empty shell while the shell with the magnet was now in my pocket.

"Guess you lose," I said, reaching for the combined packets of money.

Larry picked the shell out of my hand and turned it over to inspect it, too late, too late.

He put the duplicate ball back on the bar, ran his hand over the surface of my small table and made a slight bow in my direction. "I admit defeat."

"Wait, I'm going to celebrate by buying a round for the house Join us if you like."

"Not many customers here this time of day and I'll make one less." He was still notably confused as he walk out the door.

"See you tomorrow," the bartender jovially taunted him.

"Nevermore," he replied. "Poe's raven said it first but I mean it most." The door swung closed behind him.

"There a gimmick with that table?" the bartender ask.

"Table is very important. Important distraction."

"Do tell."

"Well everybody," I spoke loudly to be heard throughout the room, "next rounds on me. Victory celebration. Take it out of this," I continued, facing the bartender, pulling the top bill out of Larry's packet within the red rubber band.

The bartender started to ring up the estimated charge for refueling the house and stopped with the twenty in front of his face. He looked at the bill carefully. "This is no good."

"What?"

"Counterfeit."

"Damn. Well, take it out of one of my twenties." As I pulled the top bill out of my packet I was surprised to find that the next bill was only a ten. I knew what the bartender was going to say just seconds before he spoke again.

"This is no good either."

"I can't believe he switched it. Only out of my hand for a second while he put a rubber band around it."

"That guy is really good," the bartender gushed in admiration, oblivious to any discomfort that the remark might cause me.

"He ever done that before?"

"Never lost a bet before."

"You know Larry's last name?"

"No," the bartender grinned shaking his head. "Maybe he didn't want to take a chance that someone might want to identify him. Or being involved in an illegal game of chance."

"Any idea where he lives?"

"I'm sure you know the answer to that already."

"Call me when he shows up again," I requested, sliding a business card across to him.

"I think he's apt to keep that vow of never darkening our already dimly lit lounge again. Fear of being caught."

"What's your name, by the way?"

"Why do you ask?"

"I sometime write up my experiences as short stores and my editor complains about lack of naming characters and describing them."

"You have a wise editor. My name is Bert and I look just average."

"Okay, Bert, thanks."

As I was passing through the doorway, I heard Bert asking, "And what's your name?"

I didn't answer because I didn't want to take a chance on

being questioned about an illegal gambling operation or of proclaiming myself a fool when this story hit the internet. Larry was probably pretty sure that I wouldn't be reporting anything about the situation for that reason.

Looking back. Bert had my business card under examination and I was pleased that he had a chance to read the description of my occupation which was "Prestidigitator" in very small print in the center before itself destructed and left only the number of an answering service and address of a mail receiving concern as a clue to my identity.

TECHNOLOGY SHOWDOWN IN YINGYANG CITY, NEVADA

By Edward Riepe

"Where did you get this Free America flag, Senior?" asked Alice.

"Your mom gave it to me after I rode Spooky at Sin City Prison. I have carried it with me a long time but I have never used it."

"She gave one of her flags…to you? Sure she did. Just like she gave you that kiss and I will be damned. This is one of her flags! It has the words 'Bite Me' in big white letters embroidered on both sides. Those flags are rare," added Alexis.

"Sort of, I reckon. Since that droid seems to know where everyone is at, ask her where Crazy Louise is right now?"

There was a brief pause before Marsha reported.

"She is sitting in a chair in a room located on the top floor in the southeast corner of her casino with a pair of binoculars. She is alone for the moment."

"I have been in that casino many times and I know what she looks like. What if I snuck in there and kidnapped her alive while everyone is distracted? I think I could pull that off and I am dressed for the occasion," he asked with a wicked smile on his face.

"That would be wonderful. What about the remaining members of the Monster Squad? How do we handle that? We are not familiar with the layout of the town or the casino," said Wiley Junior.

"Frank and I will stay with Alice while she rigs up her flag and you two act like you are returning to the Sliver ranch. Once you are out of sight behind this ridge head into the woods to our west. Surely there are trails in those woods that can get you to the alley behind the China Doll Casino. Leave Junior to guard the horses while you try to do your thing, Senior. Does this woman know you well?" asked Alexis.

"She might remember me but the last time we got frisky was five or six years ago. She is good looking woman for her age but I don't think she will be a problem. Everyone will be standing at the windows watching the showdown and if anyone recognizes me on this ridge they will just think I am returning to my church to avoid any trouble. Trust me. I will show you youngsters new meaning when people talk about the old in and out when it comes to kidnapping. Let's go, Junior. Wait! Could I borrow one of your Colts with a silencer, just in case?"

Alice removed the Colt hanging off the left side of her upper body and removed a silencer from her right saddlebag and handed both to Senior.

"If you don't think she will be a problem why do you need my silencer? Your church? What do you mean by that?" asked Alexis.

Wiley Senior laughed.

"Everyone in this town who knows me thinks I'm a roaming man of God traveling from town to town to preach when I am wearing this suit. Most bounty hunters never make it out of this town because of the gold they carry. I guess you couldn't read that in my thoughts because those are good memories. As for Lou, I think she will be happy to see me alone in that room. If she goes into Crazy Louise mode I will shoot one of her hands so she can at least walk away with me. Sound good to you?"

"I reckon. Be careful. It is loaded and ready to fire, daddy in law. Don't get yourself killed. We need you to show us the way to San Francisco," added Alexis.

"You do the same. Alice, I take it this will be like the firing line this morning with the drone?" asked Senior.

"Her name is Marsha. Yes is the answer," answered Alice.

"Just remember this, like Zak used to say. Fight dirty because there are no rules. When that ark moves in and if he gets distracted by that or if he gets distracted by the laser fire coming out of nowhere, plug him then. Don't let him beat you to the draw. I hear he is pretty fast. That is my sermon for today."

"I will remember that. Now go because time is slipping by."

The McFosters turned their horses and headed towards the Sliver ranch. Once they were behind the ridge from prying eyes they moved into the nearby woods.

"This is about the most hair brained idea I have ever been a part of, although Senior has been pretty creative the last two years with some of his plans. Why don't you walk into town and leave your horse here? I will dismount and move off to the side of the trail along with Frank. I can use the horses to cover my actions. I will have my Winchester ready to use just in case he gets lucky. Mom is gonna' be pissed off if she finds out about this, especially if you get seriously hurt or killed. At this distance, I can pick off his ear with that rifle," said Alexis.

"Yeah, but we want to help out Frank when it comes to earning the people's trust and everyone will know we are Free America scouts when I plant that flag in the street. They all know that we are the good guys. That might be a good idea with your Winchester but I think Marsha can handle it but go ahead anyway. Five hundred thousand years of technology is great but you can't beat old west technology when it comes to rifles. Let's get this over with."

Alice took her time attaching the Free America flag to her improvised flag pole and during that time her mind was flooded with messages from her sister, the McFosters and Frank.

Suddenly there was an unfamiliar voice in her mind.

"We have arrived and are waiting on your command."

"Who was that?" asked Alexis turning to face Frank while she was placing the barrel of her Winchester on the surface of her saddle.

"That was my bonded mate, Donna. She is the best pilot in Heaven Incorporated when it comes to the ark class of starships.

We can't see the Sanctuary Ark for the moment because it is cloaked but believe me it is right in front of our eyes."

Alice began her walk towards the Chuluota Kid carrying her mother's Free America flag bearing the words 'Bite Me'. She found herself slightly anxious but she had a strange calm come over her emotions. When she reached the first commercial building on Fourth Street she paused and looked at the building. The sign read 'Shaker's Hardware Store'. Then the rain started to fall again. This time it was between a drizzle and a driving rain. She threw her rain poncho on her back to reveal her three guns. She had used her fourth holster, which was empty, to hold the butt of her flagpole while she walked.

She thrust the flagpole into the Nevada mud and was surprised at how easy that task was.

"All targets acquired save for one," she heard in her head.

Alice wondered where Marsha was located. She looked up briefly above her head towards the rain clouds to see if she could see the telltale sign of water running off her hull and saw nothing but raindrops. The cold rain felt good on her face. After lowering her head for the protection her scout hat offered she began to walk faster towards her target which seemed like a short walk. She stopped when she was forty feet away. What she saw surprised her. The Chuluota Kid was young, at least no older than Trey and he was wearing a baseball cap.

He looked like a punk.

"I need your guns if you want to go any further up Fourth

Street," yelled the Kid for all the townspeople to hear.

The elevated wooden sidewalks were packed with people who had spilled out of the stores, bars and whorehouses that lined Fourth Street.

"Then you have a problem. No one takes my guns away from me and that includes you."

"You are young. Why are you here?"

"For you, punk."

"I don't kill women but I can make an exception to that rule just for you."

"We know that is not true. So you are not only a punk you are a liar as well. You are a brave little boy when you have your nine buddies backing you up but today that won't help you. How many of those one hundred and thirteen people you say you have killed were because of you? I can tell from your face it has been nine, nine old men. I am not an old man. Make your move. Come on, punk. It's time you took a chance for once. After all, I am just a woman and you just murdered two unarmed girls. Take a chance with one wearing a Colt 1911 on her hip, little boy," stated Alice.

At that moment nine white streaks of light flashed in the air just behind the Chuluota Kid from twenty feet above. The sound created by the invisible droid was similar to the sizzle of lightening when it strikes too close but there was no accompanying clap of thunder.

At the same moment the Sanctuary Ark dropped her cloak to

reveal to everyone how large the hovering black ship was. The ark dwarfed the town and looked out of place so close to the surface of Lake Tahoe.

There was silence for at least two seconds with only the sound of the rain impacting the puddle laden ground. Then there were screams and shouts from the townspeople who were now scrambling to get inside any building. The Kid turned to see what was grabbing everyone's attention. He maintained that gaze for a long five seconds and took two steps back before he regained his composure.

"What is she doing, Alex? Shoot! Shoot him, Alice!" exclaimed Frank.

"That's just Alice," answered Alex while looking through her scope.

She had a smile on her face. She already knew this fight was about to end on a good note.

Finally the Chuluota Kid turned slowly to face Alice.

"I bet you don't like that show. I brought my friends along for this ride to make it a fair fight. I have seen that look on scared little boys when I was growing up but that won't work on me. Make your move...punk!" demanded Alice.

The Kid quickly moved his right hand to the gun on his hip. He heard a shot ring out but he could no longer feel his hand. He looked down to see that a bullet had ripped off his fingers. He looked up to see Alice walking towards him with her Colt leveled at his head and the end of the barrel was smoking.

Another shot rang out connecting on his right knee. He fell to his right landing in large puddle of mud that was four inches deep. While lying in the mud he started to verbalize.

"Help me! Somebody help me! Somebody, anybody kill her!" he cried out.

Within seconds Alice was standing over him in the puddle with her Colt still leveled at his face.

"I knew I was faster than you. I could have killed you easily but I wanted it to be a fair fight. That is more than you gave all those poor souls who faced you before. I just have one question. How does it feel knowing you are about to die?" she asked coldly.

"Who are you? Are you a Free America scout?"

"You got one thing right in your miserable life."

Alice sent her third bullet through his forehead and the Kid slumped over face down in the muddy puddle.

"So much for punks running loose in Nevada," she said softly.

JACKPOT OR THE ART OF LIVING

By Jay Hill

The first thing my wife said to me was, "I'll get a towel. You're getting blood all over the place."

She didn't give a shit about me bleeding. It was the mess she wanted to avoid.

She threw the towel at me. She was wearing her work uniform and didn't want to get it bloody. I reached for the towel and passed out.

Later, much later, when I could laugh about it, I told people that we celebrated our anniversary with a bang.

I came to in the hospital. A nurse summoned a doctor. The doc said, "We need your permission to operate, to get the bullet out of you. Normally, your wife could give it, but given the circumstances, we can't use her and, anyway, she's with the police right now."

I said, "What's the alternative?"

"You can leave as 'refused medical treatment' and 'against medical advice.' The wound is almost certainly infected, it will get worse, gangrene will set in, and you'll die of septic shock."

"The way things have been going that might not be so bad."

The doc didn't smile. He was the kind of over-serious, wimpy bastard who wouldn't know a joke if it fucked him. I looked at the nurse standing next to him. She looked more annoyed and angry than the doc. She was matronly and overweight. I figured she was probably irritable because she wasn't getting any. It ran through my head to tell her to pick up a vibrator on the way home, but I decided to be a gentleman about it. I reached out and touched her wrist. It was cold as ice. I knew that second that the hospital was populated by the sort of douche bags that trade their souls for a paycheck.

"It was a joke -- sort of," I said in my most pitiful voice. Then in a moment of faux depression, self-pity, and an attempt to grift the doc, "My whole fucking life's been one long fucking joke."

It didn't work.

"I don't have time for your jokes," the doc said, "this is your life. If you want to die, I've got an ER full of patients who want to live."

That took it down to the brass tacks. Hell, I wanted to live.

I told the doc the short, and more or less truthful, version what happened. He said, "You're lucky she shot you where she did."

"It took her two shots to hit me," I said. "If I'd had the gun and been that close to her, I would have blown her shit away. The fucking bitch. When I get better, I'm going to beat her like a dog and then I'm going to beat her some more until I feel good about the day."

The doc turned and walked out — the wimpy fucking bastard.

I was bullshitting him, and he didn't get that I was ripping off Robert Johnson's "Me and the Devil Blues," but the fucker still couldn't see the joke so fuck him again.

Two female police officers from the domestic violence unit visited me in the hospital. One was a cadet officer who tagged along with the real officer. The officer acted pissed that I didn't want to press charges, but I thought her anger wasn't genuine.

"She'll probably kill you the next time," she said. "Our experience is that domestic violence situations escalate until they're terminated by divorce, jail or death."

The cadet had a baby-face with big, puffy dick-sucking lips and, despite her bullet proof vest, I could tell she had nice tits. I wondered if her labia were as swollen as I imagined, how big her nips were, and if her pussy was a cock-crusher. I fantasized that she drove around in a squad car doing Kegel exercises all day and getting horny. I saw that police officer looked like a bull dyke, and I realized that the two of them were probably getting it on. What a waste of good pussy, maybe world class pussy.

"I'm through with the bitch," I said, but I knew I wasn't. I figured I deserved what I got for letting her sister blow me on our anniversary. It wasn't a very smart thing to do. I should have waited for some other day. That's what a better man, a man with different goals in life, would have done, but I didn't want to be a "better man."

My goal in life, and what I put down to have printed in my high school yearbook, but was censored out, was to have as many orgasms as I could before I died, but this episode was making me realize that I didn't want to die for an orgasm.

I explained to the officer what happened and how once her sister got me hard, I couldn't help myself. I was in the grip of an irresistible impulse or at least an irresistible grip. I thought she'd understand and she'd think it was funny.

Instead, she looked hard at me. "Is your name really .... Seymour Anus Haney?"

The cadet got a silly, stupid fucking grin on her face like she'd just farted.

I looked at the cadet. "What the fuck's wrong with you?"

"Nothing," she said. She turned her back to me, and I could tell she was laughing.

"What about the name?" the officer asked.

My mother said that my name was my father's doing, that he took care of the name registration and told her that he was drunk at the time from celebrating my birth. She said he thought it was a joke at the time, but he later sometimes said he regretted it, though at other times he said it would toughen me up. So, if you believe my mother, this man who died when I was six months old, fucked up my whole life as a joke. I thought they were both in on it.

"Yeah, my parents thought it was a hoot, but then they were assholes."

"You shouldn't talk about your parents like that."

"What are you now, the goddam 'respect-your-parents' police?"

"No, but I can sap you in the balls hard enough to make you wish I were. - Now, what about your name?"

Whacking my nuts seemed to be the go to answer to every question that day.

"My parents should have given me a normal name. Can you imagine what it was like in high school? Can you imagine what it was like in the Army?"

I went on, "The first day in basic training we sat around in what was the Army's version of a big circle jerk and our drill sergeant gave each of us some shit. It was like he was doing an insult comedian routine, but you pay to see a comedian, and I would have paid to see the drill sergeant go away. When he came to me, he said, 'How the fuck did you get a name like Seymour Anus Haney?'

"I naive enough to think he wanted a serious response and said, 'My parents were fucking jokesters, a million fucking laughs, and thank you for letting everybody know.'

"The drill sergeant said, 'Give me twenty-five.'

"I said, 'What the fuck for!'

"He said, 'Make it seventy-five.'

"When I got done, the drill sergeant said, 'You're a fuck-up Anus, but we're going give you a new Army name with the hope that it will inspire you to asshole greatness.' He laughed at his own joke, the dumb fucker. 'From now on we're going to call you 'Fuzz Nuts.' He looked around the circle. 'I don't ever want to hear any of you maggots call Anus, here, anything other than 'Fuzz Nuts' the rest of the time you maggots are in basic.'

"My platoon shortened it to 'Fuzzy,' and the nickname stuck with me until I was discharged for being 'unable to adapt to the military way of life' which meant the Army was so tired of my fuck-ups that it was more convenient to get rid of me than put up with me. So, for your information officer, I've had two fucking inspirational names in my life, and neither one worked out worth a shit."

The police officer rolled her eyes. She rubbed her tongue against her cheek like it was a dog's tail wagging and open mouth grinned. "Maybe the next time your wife will put a bullet up your middle name." She started laughing like she was the first person who ever made a joke about my name. She immediately went on my lifetime list of fucking moron douche bags.

"You can't talk to the public like that. You're paid to respect people."

She said, "You don't like it, go file a complaint . . . asshole." She and the cadet started laughing hard. They put their arms around each other and walked away still shaking from laughter and without even saying, "Goodbye." The officer let her right hand slip down, and she played grab ass with the cadet's left butt cheek.

I yelled, "Asshole, yourself." The police officer stopped in the doorway and looked back.

She said, "You were lucky she's a bad shot. Maybe I'll take her to the range. I think I will."

They walked away laughing harder.

Women all hang together. It's so unfair. I mean, I was a victim. I was a crime victim. I was shot, and because it was all women, they thought it was a joke.

They kept me in the hospital a few more days than necessary. I think it was to milk my health insurance so when I told them I couldn't pay the deductible, they'd have made enough on bullshit charges to write the balance off.

I found that there were the statutory-max fifteen video poker machines in the gift shop and that, when you've got your arm in a sling and you tell the truth about how you were shot for no reason, it wasn't hard to panhandle twenty bucks off some geriatric rube who felt sorry for you.

I found it helped if I told them I was all religious and stuff like that and it helped without end if I said that I saw Jesus at the end of the tunnel while I was unconscious. I'm not sure why that helped, but one guy gave me a hundred bucks. He said, "Son, you need to have some entertainment while you're in here." I thought about trying to call a hooker, but in the end, I got a bus driver who was on break to blow me in a broom closet for twenty bucks. I think the guy who gave me the money would have been proud of my frugality.

None of it would have happened if my wife hadn't opened her eyes right after she swallowed. Instead of looking at me, she looked down and saw the lipstick on my underwear.

"What the fuck is that?" she said.

She had some leakage running from her lip to her chin. It was hard to take her seriously.

I said, "You must have brushed up against me when you pulled my underwear down."

She took advantage of me laying back in the chair and her being down on her knees in front of me. She jerked up on my dick so hard; I thought she ripped it off. She slapped my nuts like a tetherball and followed with an uppercut fist to my perineum that could have knocked out Jack Dempsey. She dragged me out of the chair by my nuts and started kicking at my crotch. I curled up in a defensive position and protected my privates with my hands.

She stood over me like that giant woman sci-fi movie character. "I work all day on our anniversary and come home to this. — You piece of shit."

She walked out of the room. I was afraid she was going to go Bobbitt on me and try to cut off my nuts or my dick. I didn't know she went for my gun. I lay there praying the pain would go away and hoping she would too.

I did promise God that if he got me through this, I'd devote my life to him, but I later retracted that promise based on my attorney's advice that promises made under duress were not enforceable and could be revoked. I did not explain the whole situation exactly straight to my attorney so I could be in cosmic trouble.

I was so screwed up I thought that if my wife walked out and spent the night somewhere else, it would save the cost an anniversary dinner, but in hindsight, by that time, anniversary dinner wasn't happening.

We lived "separate and apart," as the temporary restraining order described it, until we went to court, and I asked for the domestic violence charge to be dismissed. I showed the judge a letter from the trailer park showing that we'd paid for the damages for repairing the hole in our trailer and the one next to ours, but he didn't seem to care about that.

Before the hearing, my wife said, "It wouldn't have surprised me if it was my mother. She'll fuck anything that resembles a hard dick, but I thought my sister had more class."

It showed how little my wife knew about her family. Her sister will do any a mammal with hard on. As for her mother, the MILF next door told me that my mother-in-law likes to wear a strap-on and be the one doing the fucking. No wonder the old man is such a grouch.

After the hearing, we went back to the trailer park, and my wife and her sister got into a fight. My wife lost a tooth which I thought was a more noticeable disfigurement than my scar.

A month later, I told my wife I wanted to have her name tattooed in a multi-colored heart over my heart. She volunteered to have my initials tattooed on her right ass cheek in the style of a branding. After we discussed it with the tattoo artist and agreed on a price, we went out to the car and smoked a joint.

Even though I was still milking the clinic for pain pills from the shooting, I didn't want to feel any pain, and it looked like a good excuse for a quickie, so I asked my wife if she'd blow me before we went back in to get the tattoos.

"After the joint and with the endorphins from a fresh orgasm, I don't think I'd be feeling any pain from the needle."

"You are an asshole."

That hurt, coming from her.

I said, "I like to think of myself as a 'deplorable' and that it's just my version of pussy grabbing and you know, that's all been normalized. On top of that, if you want me to, I'll finger you in the back seat."

"You're serious? You want me to do that?"

"I don't know whether you know this or not, but semen has an analgesic quality, so it's as much for you as for me. You'll get pain relief, too."

I've never understood whether she's dumb, gullible or submissive, but I know she's the best.

I thought my brother-in-law might kill me, but my sister-in-law never told him what happened and when she turned up pregnant, he got all sentimental about having a kid and forgot about the problems my wife and I had and, in any event, he didn't make the connection. My wife said that she'd tell him except she'd probably wind up paying child support after paying my funeral expenses.

I figured the truth was that my brother-in-law and his wife were the only ones in the family that didn't live in a trailer and might be able to take us in if we ever got broke and that no matter how irresponsible my wife was with the whole gun thing and getting all overly emotional and acting impulsively and all that, that she didn't want to risk losing her brother-in-law as a safety net.

My father-in-law was a mean prick who never cracked a smile. We were over at his double-wide one day, I was sitting in a chair watching Springer on the TV, and the old bastard got semi-sober long enough to get up in my face and call me bitches and whores.

"You're a real cocksucker, you know. You're probably the most despicable son-of-a-bitch I've ever met. How a low down, good for nothing, freeloader like you talked my daughter into marrying him, I'll never know."

He was acting like such a jerk. - I decided to egg him on.

"It isn't PC or nice to call people cocksuckers and, anyway, I don't suck cock. I think your son might - you might want to check with him about that. I do eat your daughter's pussy and most the other pussies in your family except for your wife. I wouldn't eat your wife's pussy because I think she's saving up for a sex change if she hasn't already had one."

The old bastard was quicker than I thought he could be, in his semi-drunk condition. He snap-punched me in the face and broke my nose.

I screamed like hell.

My wife came from the kitchen and glassed her father with a half empty beer bottle. He fell to the floor. Blood poured from the back of his head.

"You want to know why I married him?" she said. "I'll tell you why: He had the biggest cock in my high school class, and, you know what? I ought to know because I sucked all of them trying to escape you and your pervy strap-on queen."

The old man sat up and started to cry. I was never so proud of my wife, standing up to her father like that, and it was then that I understood why she got back together with me, and why she was so jealous of her sister.

It took fourteen stitches at the local health clinic to close the cut to in the old bastard's bald spot. They fixed my nose, and with a fake ID and stolen credit card, I signed as the financially responsible party. Since they can't find me, the bill collectors are hounding the old man. I hope they repo the motherfucker's scalp.

Blood stains, some mine, some his, all over his carpet from the incident. They'll probably withhold enough to pay for a new carpet from his deposit when he moves or dies. That's a hoot because the carpet was worn out when he moved in.

I lost my blackjack dealer gig, but I didn't give a damn. It was a cheap ass third rate casino populated by locals that didn't toke worth a shit, and I hated the pit bosses, and the job sucked in general. The only good thing about it was a bottle-blonde nympho who worked the same shift two days a week, but she didn't want to do anything other than pussy-fuck, and that got to be boring long before I got shot.

I went back to my old casino once. I walked through the front door, and my old pit boss was standing there. It turned out that he'd been promoted to floor-manager and was looking at some slot machines near the door. He hugged me and made over me like I was the projectile son or something and told me how much he missed me and how I was one of the best workers he ever had.

The whole time he was going on, I kept thinking: You lousy motherfucker - you rotten no good son of a bitch. You were such a dick to me the whole time I worked here. Then I told him what a great boss he was and how much I missed him. He ate that shit up, and after enough of that love fest, I began to wonder if he was lying to me as much as I was lying to him because he never said why don't you come back to work or put in an application or something.

I roamed around the casino and saw a lot of my old friends and a lot of my not-so-much friends, but fellow workers. I was impressed with how happy everyone seemed until I realized that we all looked that way and that they were all really unhappy and only looked like that to get better tokes.

After a while, I sat down and started to play some five dollar blackjack and as sooner as I started, security showed up and told me that my play wasn't welcome and gave me a trespass warning which meant that if I ever go back, they'll arrest me. So fuck the whole bunch of sons of bitches and especially my old pit boss who must have arranged the trespass thing. He always was a worthless piece of shit and always will be.

One morning at unemployment, I ran into a couple of girls I knew from high school. One of them was still living at home, and her parents were out of town. I went home, got my stash, and the three of us partied all afternoon at her house. They had the same sort of bad luck after high school that I had with jobs and bosses. I think the girls had probably turned a few tricks, something I'm proud that I can say I've never done.

I got home late, and my wife was waiting. She was pissed. She accused me of cheating on her and called me an asshole a few times, but I had learned to keep my underwear clean, and by the next morning she was back at doing her Hoover imitation. She is the best.

I needed some transportation while I was looking for work, so I borrowed money from my brother-in-law and bought a used moped. I cruised the Fremont Street area and picked up a chippy who was too young to gamble but the perfect age for fucking. She was so ignorant she didn't know what "blasé" meant and she thought "irregardless" was a word. She thought blasé meant something like et cetera or et al. When I told her that I had some weed but no ecstasy, she told me that she was "ready to party, irregardless, blasé, blasé." Well, I was ready to blasé her tight, young pussy so I could overlook her ignorance and lack of class.

We were on my scooter and headed to a friend's apartment on the East side when the chippy lowered her hand and began rubbing my dick. I got distracted and ran a red light, and a car clipped the tail of the moped. I got road rash, but the chippy got her leg under the moped, and it bled like a motherfucker. The last time I saw the chippy, she was being hauled off to the hospital. Since we hadn't hooked up, and she was a bit young, I figured she wouldn't want to see me.

There weren't any witnesses, and I told the cops I thought the light was green. I wasn't cited, but the moped was totaled. I told the other driver that I thought the Bible said lawsuits were un-Christian. I caught a bus home and smoked a blunt to calm my nerves.

When my brother-in-law heard what happened and offered to loan me the money to buy another scooter. He said I could pay him back when I got a job. He assumed I needed a scooter for work transportation. He didn't need to know that it was more likely that I'd use it to come over and get a blow job from his wife and fuck her a few times while he was ass-kissing the system making money to loan to me.

Two weeks after the accident the cops raided our trailer but by that time I was into the pain medication from the surgery, and they didn't find anything except for an old bong. The next month I got a letter from a lawyer who said he represented the girl and her parents and with a lot of big legal words said he was going to sue my ass off and recommended that I forward his letter to my insurer. Right, my insurer. What a hoot. I used his letter for t.p.

About a month later, I got a second letter from the attorney. It said that said he'd sent me the first letter and that ignoring his letters wouldn't make the matter go away. About a month after the second letter, a PI showed up at the door. When I told him I didn't have any insurance, he said that I could lose my license if I couldn't pay for the girl's injuries. What license?

At the trial, the girl showed up looking like the Virgin Mary, dressed in a school uniform: a blue pleated skirt, a white blouse, black shoes and a blue blazer with a crest. She used white knee socks to cover her prothesis. When she took it off to show the scar to the judge, she gave the whole courtroom a first rate crotch shot of her pink panties. I think she did it for the benefit of the judge.

She finished "test-i-lying," and the judge said he had some questions for her in private. The Judge asked the parents' attorney if he objected to the girl giving testimony in chambers and he said no. The black robed son of a bitch never asked me for my permission, and I didn't realize until later that if I had objected, he couldn't do that. The judge and the girl spent about an hour in the judge's chamber. They came out with huge shit eating, guilty grins on their faces and I knew I was fucked.

To keep from thinking about the fact that my case going down the shitter, I started thinking about how the girl looked so very fuckable in her school uniform getup and all and she was over sixteen by the time of the trial and the whole time she was on the witness stand, I kept thinking I've never had a one-legged one. It was like my life was being arranged by some cosmic force to allow me to fulfill that fantasy.

I must have leered at the girl some because her father got me in the hallway outside the courtroom and said that if I kept looking at her like I was that he'd beat the shit out of me for that and for crippling his daughter and then he said that my whole useless life, as he, hardly a disinterested party, chose to describe it, wasn't worth the price he'd pay.

The mother stood there and watched with a look on her face like someone had rammed a dry corn cob up her butt. I said to her, "Are you going to stand there and let your husband threaten me?" and the expression on her face never changed. I hope she has the same expression whenever he fucks her. He probably never does, so he's just another sorry, worthless piece of shit.

The judge awarded the chippy and her parents like a gazillion dollars and called me irresponsible for not having insurance and said that I was a symbol of everything that was wrong with our society. I say, "Fuck him and the horse he rode in on," and I hope when he fucks his wife, she has the same dry corn cob up her butt look on her face as the girl's mother.

When it was all over, we all walked out into the hallway. I figured I had nothing to lose at that point, so I said to the Father, "Good luck on collecting on your judgment - dickhead," and ran like hell.

The parents and the court system and the lawyers did me a favor because, as I explained to my wife, if I got a straight job they would garnishee two-thirds of my net wages. So it didn't make sense to work at anything other than stuff that would be under the table cash and since most employers, who will pay you cash in hand, hire Hispanics and pay them some bullshit wage that requires the whole family to work in order to make ends meet and I wasn't going to do that, there wasn't much left for me to do other than to find some self-employment that was a cash only business.

The obvious thing to do was to sell dope, but I didn't like the furtive aspects of it, and I didn't like the idea of going to jail and more troubling was the fact that, while they drove the mob out of the casinos, they didn't drive the mob out of town or City Hall, so if you wanted to sell dope in Las Vegas or Clark County you needed to work with some people who might put you in a hole in the desert if you cheated them or they thought you cheated them, and I knew sooner or later I would cheat them, so I wrote off selling dope because I didn't see myself in a hole in the ground.

The newspaper gave me my big idea, my big break. It did an article on panhandlers in Las Vegas. Most of them barely get by, but about three of them make great money, I mean the best guy averages about forty-five dollars and hour and doesn't report any of that income though I wondered if after the article he got a visit from the IRS. Anyway, most of the panhandlers have some bullshit story and hold up hand made signs that say stuff like "Need Money for Bus to Phoenix" or "Have Cancer, Can't Work" or "Three Hungry Children" and most people know all these signs are not just exaggeration but complete and total fabrication; I mean these guys are lying, and everyone knows it, but some people figure if someone is so hard up that they'll hold up a sign that is an embarrassing lie that they must be desperate for some reason and give them money. These were the barely making it dudes.

The successful panhandlers didn't bullshit anybody or hold up any pathetic signs trying to play on the emotions of other people. They held up signs that said things like "Unemployed - Need Money." When people asked them why they were panhandling, they told the truth which was of course that they didn't have a job and didn't have any job prospects and people gave them money like there was no tomorrow. I thought, "Jesus Christ, what kind of qualifications are those. All you have to do is quit your job, and you're unemployed and need money," and these bozos are pulling down big donations.

So I made a sign that said, "Can't Work - Need Money." Of course, it was the absolute, honest-to-God truth. I could hold up my hand and swear to that on a stack of Bibles. If someone asked me I am ready with a spiel about how the court system fucked me over and now if I worked they were going to garnishee two-thirds of my net income and made it sound like it was going to be split between the clerk of courts and the judge.

I mean who doesn't hate the fucking court system. The average driver who goes by on the street only knows a court system that fucks them for driving a few miles an hour over the speed limit. You do like seventy in forty-five, like most the major streets are in Las Vegas, and some douche bag justice of the peace, fake, wannabe judge, lawyer-puke who paid a political party so he could put on a robe, fines you two hundred and fifty dollars and suspends your license for a year.

So now, the best thing I've got going for me is that the same court system that fucked me over because some damn Lolita-like chippie rubbed my cock and I missed a light, has given me the best grift opportunity I've had in years. I mean, I work when I want to, if I don't feel like it or the weather is bad, I stay home. I ride the scooter my brother in law paid for to work and hide it in the parking lot of a fast food joint that's on the corner. On days when I don't work, I ride it over to his place and do his wife.

And talk about women, ninety-nine percent of the women that pass by the corner I'm grifting are scared to death of panhandlers and they lock their doors when they see one, but one percent are cruising for some action, or they're desperately lonely or have some sort of a "take care of a sick puppy" obsession, and if you look like you've bathed in the last twenty-four hours, they're ready to take you home and treat you to a fresh crotch-clam or fur-burger fun meal, and, of course, I'm alway ready to provide them with tube steak.

One percent may not sound like much, but think that every day some forty thousand cars go by the corner where I work. The downside is that most of them want to give you twenty bucks and have you get all emotional over such a chicken shit little donation, but, every once in while one of them gets all sentimental herself and give you a C-note.

"Irregardless and blasé-blasé," the chippy liked to say, but I say, "Nothing ventured, nothing gained." I like to keep a positive mental attitude and look on the bright side of things, and that's how I look at everything that happened beginning with getting shot on my anniversary and ending with my entry into career panhandling.

I make more take-home money now than I did at the casino. I work three days a week and have a lot more time for pussy hunting. You might think it's a bitch when it rains, but people feel sorry for some poor guy out in the rain, and I make money out the wazoo on rainy days. It's like I got the world by the tail.

You've just got to have that old American entrepreneurial spirit and take the rubes for everything they've got. And so, that's my gig in the gig economy.

I represent the finest, the most heroic and glorious aspects of American culture. I'm out there every day putting it all on the pass line, living the presidentially endorsed American dream, and grabbing 'em by the pussy. I am the new cowboy, the lonesome rider, a modern paladin fighting the injustices visited on me by a rigged economic system, and, along the way, I provide an important service to the women I encounter, especially those who need a little strange or are married to some dipshit who doesn't know how to satisfy a woman, how to show one that you really care for her, or just doesn't have the time.

Look for me on a corner near you.